Treasure Island

Treasure Island

Abridged from the original by
Robert Louis Stevenson

Illustrations by
Francesca Greco

CD narrated by
Jasper Britton

SOURCEBOOKS
Jabberwocky
AN IMPRINT OF SOURCEBOOKS

Published by Sourcebooks Jabberwocky, an imprint of Sourcebooks, Inc.
P.O. Box 4410, Naperville, Illinois 60567-4410
(630) 961-3900
Fax: (630) 961-2168
www.sourcebooks.com

Library of Congress Cataloging-in-Publication Data

Stevenson, Robert Louis.
  Treasure Island : abridged from the original / by Robert Louis Stevenson.
    p. cm.
  CD narrated by Jasper Britton.
  Summary: An innkeeper's son finds a treasure map that leads him to a pirate's fortune
and grave danger.
  [1. Buried treasure—Fiction. 2. Pirates—Fiction. 3. Adventure and adventurers—Fiction.
4. Caribbean Area—History—18th century—Fiction.] I. Britton, Jasper. II. Title.
  PZ7.S8482 Tr 2008
  [Fic]—dc22
                            2008009133

                    Printed in China.
                OGP 10 9 8 7 6 5 4 3

Printed by: O.G. Printing Productions, Ltd., Kowloon, Hong Kong
Date of Production: 6/15/10
ID # 12717

CONTENTS

Chapter 1

BLACK DOG APPEARS AND DISAPPEARS

Squire Trelawney, Dr. Livesey, and the rest of these gentlemen having asked me to write down the whole particulars about Treasure Island, I take up my pen and go back to the time when my father kept the Admiral Benbow inn and the brown old seaman with the sabre cut first took up his lodging under our roof. I remember him looking round the cove and whistling to himself as he did so, and then breaking out in that old sea-song that he sang so often afterwards:

"Fifteen men on the dead man's chest—

Yo-ho-ho, and a bottle of rum!"

"Here you, matey," he cried to the man who trundled the barrow; "bring up alongside and help up my chest."

He was a very silent man by custom. Every day when he came back from his stroll he would ask if any seafaring men had gone by along the road. When a seaman did put up at the Admiral Benbow he would look in at him through the curtained door before he entered the parlour; and he was always sure to be as silent as a mouse when any such was present. He had taken me aside one day and promised me a silver fourpenny on the first of every month if I would only keep my "weather-eye open for a seafaring man with one leg" and let him know the moment he appeared.

His stories were what frightened people worst of all. Dreadful stories they were—about hanging, and walking the plank, and storms at sea, and the Dry Tortugas, and wild deeds and places on the Spanish Main. The great sea-chest none of us had ever seen open.

✳ ✳ ✳

It was one January morning, very early—a pinching, frosty morning. The captain had risen earlier than usual and set out down the beach, his cutlass swinging under the broad skirts of the old blue coat, his brass telescope under his arm, his hat tilted back upon his head.

The parlour door opened and a man stepped in on whom I had never set my eyes before. He was a pale, tallowy creature, wanting two fingers of the left hand, and though he wore a cutlass, he did not look much like a fighter. He was not sailorly, and yet he had a smack of the sea about him too.

I asked him what was for his service, and he said he would take rum; but as I was going out of the room to fetch it, he sat down upon a table and motioned me to draw near.

"Is this here table for my mate Bill? He has a cut on one cheek and a mighty pleasant way with him, particularly in drink, has my mate Bill. Now, is Bill in this here house?"

I told him he was out walking.

At last in strode the captain, slammed the door behind him, without looking to the right or left, and marched straight across the room to where his breakfast awaited him.

"Bill," said the stranger in a voice that I thought he had tried to make bold and big. The captain spun round on his heel and fronted us.

"Black Dog!" said he.

"And who else?" returned the other.

"Now, look here," said the captain; "you've run me down; here I am; well, then, speak up; what is it?"

"We'll sit down, if you please, and talk square, like old shipmates."

He bade me go and leave the door wide open. "None of your keyholes for me, sonny," he said; and I left them together and retired into the bar.

Then all of a sudden there was a tremendous explosion of oaths and other noises—the chair and table went over in a lump, a clash of steel followed, and then a cry of pain, and the next instant I saw Black Dog in full flight, and the captain hotly pursuing, both with drawn cutlasses, and the former streaming blood from the left shoulder. The captain passed his hand over his eyes several times and at last turned back into the house.

"Jim," says he, "rum"; and as he spoke, he reeled a little, and caught himself with one hand against the wall. "Rum," he repeated. "I must get away from here. Rum!"

I ran to fetch it, but I heard a loud fall in the parlour, and running in, beheld the captain lying full length upon the floor. At the same instant my mother,

alarmed by the cries and fighting, came running downstairs to help me. Between us we raised his head. He was breathing

very loud and hard, but his eyes were closed and his face a horrible colour. It was a happy relief for us when the door opened and Doctor Livesey came in, on his visit to my father.

"Oh, doctor," we cried, "what shall we do? Where is he wounded?"

"Wounded!" said the doctor. "No more wounded than you or I. The man has had a stroke, I warned him. He should lie for a week where he is—that's the best thing for him and you; but another stroke would settle him."

About noon I stopped at the captain's door with some cooling drinks and medicines.

"Jim," he said, "you saw that seafaring man today? He's a bad un; but there's worse that put him on. Now, if I can't get away no-how, and they tip me the black spot, mind you, it's my old sea-chest they're after; you get on a horse—and go to that eternal doctor swab, and tell him to pipe all hands—magistrates and sich—and he'll lay 'em aboard at the <u>Admiral Benbow</u>—all old Flint's crew, man and boy, all on 'em that's left. I was first mate, I was, and I'm the on'y one as knows the place. He gave it me at Savannah, when he lay a-dying. But you won't peach unless they get the black spot on me, or unless you see that <u>Black Dog</u> again or a seafaring man with one leg, Jim—him above all."

"But what is the black spot, captain?" I asked.

"That's a summons, mate. I'll tell you if they get that. But you keep your weather-eye open, Jim, and I'll share with you equals, upon my honour."

Probably I should have told the whole story to the doctor, for I was in mortal fear lest the captain should repent of his confessions and make an end of me. But as things fell out, my poor father died quite suddenly that evening, which put all other matters on one side.

TRACK 2

Chapter 2

THE SEA-CHEST

The day after the funeral, and about three o'clock of a bitter, foggy, frosty afternoon, I was standing at the door for a moment, full of sad thoughts about my father, when I saw someone drawing slowly near along the road. He stopped a little from the inn, and raising his voice in an odd sing-song, addressed the air in front of him, "Will any kind friend inform a poor blind man, who has lost the precious sight of his eyes in the gracious defence of his native country, England, where or in what part of this country he may now be?"

"You are at the Admiral Benbow, Black Hill Cove, my good man," said I. I held out my hand, and the horrible, soft-spoken, eyeless creature gripped it in a moment like a vice.

"Now, boy," he said, "take me in to the captain."

I began to obey him at once, walking straight in at the door and towards the parlour, where our sick old buccaneer was sitting, dazed with rum. The poor captain raised his eyes, and at one look the rum went out of him and left him staring sober.

"Now, Bill, sit where you are," said the beggar, and I saw him pass something from the hollow of the hand that held his stick into the palm of the captain's, which closed upon it instantly.

"And now that's done," said the blind man; and with incredible accuracy and nimbleness, skipped out of the parlour and into the road.

It was some time before either I or the captain seemed to gather our senses, but at length he drew in his hand and looked sharply into the palm.

"Ten o'clock!" he cried. "Six hours. We'll do them yet," and he sprang to his feet. Even as he did so, he reeled, put his hand to his throat, stood swaying for a moment, and then, with a peculiar sound, fell from his whole height face foremost to the floor. The captain had been struck dead by thundering apoplexy.

* * *

I lost no time, of course, in telling my mother all that I knew and we saw ourselves at once in a difficult and dangerous position. It occurred to us at last to go forth together and seek help in the neighbouring hamlet.

The short and the long of the matter was, that while we could get several who were willing enough to ride to Dr. Livesey's, which lay in another direction, not one would help us to defend the inn. When each had said his say, my mother made them a speech. "If none of the rest of you dare," she said, "Jim and I dare. Back we will go, the way we came, and small thanks to you big, hulking, chicken-hearted men. We'll have that chest open, if we die for it. And I'll thank you for that bag, Mrs. Crossley, to bring back our lawful money in."

We slipped back along the hedges, till, to our relief, the door of the Admiral Benbow had

closed behind us. I slipped the bolt at once, and we stood and panted for a moment in the dark, alone in the house with the dead captain's body. On the floor close to his hand there was a little round of paper, blackened

on the one side. I could not doubt
that this was the BLACK SPOT;
and taking it up, I found written on
the other side, in a very good, clear
hand, this short message: "You have
till ten tonight."

Our old clock began striking
but the news was good, for it was
only six.

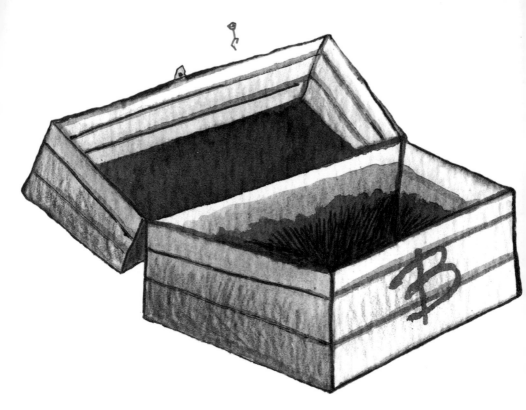

"Now, Jim," she said, "the key. Perhaps it's round his neck."

I tore open his shirt at the neck, and there, sure enough, hanging to a bit of tarry string, we found the key and hurried upstairs.

"Give me the key," said my mother; and though the lock was very stiff, she had turned it and thrown back the lid in a twinkling. A strong smell of tobacco and tar rose from the interior and there lay before us a bundle tied up in oilcloth, and looking like papers, and a canvas bag that gave forth, at a touch, the jingle of gold.

"I'll show these rogues that I'm an honest woman," said my mother. "I'll have my dues, and not a farthing over."

"And I'll take this to square the count," said I, picking up the oilskin packet.

Next moment we were both groping downstairs, leaving the candle by the empty chest; and the next we had opened the door and were in full retreat. Far less than half-way to the hamlet, very little beyond the bottom of the hill, the sound of several footsteps running came to our ears.

Three men ran together, hand in hand; and I made out, even through the mist, that the middle man of this trio was the blind beggar. The next moment his voice showed me that I was right.

"Down with the door!" he cried.

Four or five of them obeyed at once, two remaining on the road with the formidable beggar. There was a pause, then a cry of surprise, and then a voice shouting from the house, "Bill's dead. They've been before us. Someone's turned the chest out alow and aloft."

"It's these people of the inn—it's that boy. Scatter, lads, and find 'em."

Another sound then came from the top of the hill on the side of the hamlet—the tramp of horses galloping. The buccaneers turned at once and ran, separating in every direction, so that in half a minute not a sign of them remained but Pew. He remained behind, tapping up and down the road in a frenzy, and groping and calling for his comrades. Just then the noise of horses topped the rise, and four or five riders came in sight in the moonlight and swept at full gallop down the slope. At this Pew saw his error, turned with a scream, and ran straight for the ditch, into which he rolled. But he was on his feet again in a second and made another dash, now utterly bewildered, right under the nearest of the coming horses.

Chapter 3

I GO TO BRISTOL

I leaped to my feet and hailed the riders. One, tailing out behind the rest, was a lad that had gone from the hamlet to Dr. Livesey's; the rest were revenue officers. Some news of the lugger in Kitts Hole had found its way to Supervisor Dance, and set him forth in our direction. I went back with him to the Admiral Benbow, and you cannot imagine a house in such a state of smash.

"Well, then, Hawkins, what in fortune were they after?"

"I believe I have the thing in my breast pocket; and to tell you the truth, I should like to get it put in safety."

"To be sure, boy; quite right," said he. "I'll take it, if you like."

"I thought perhaps Dr. Livesey—" I began.

"Perfectly right," he interrupted very cheerily, "a gentleman and a magistrate. And, now I come to think of it, I might as well ride round there myself and report to him or squire. Now, I'll tell you, Hawkins, if you like, I'll take you along."

We rode hard all the way till we drew up before Dr. Livesey's door. Mr. Dance told me to jump down and knock.

"Is Dr. Livesey in?" I asked.

"No," said the maid, he had come home in the afternoon but had gone up to the hall to dine and pass the evening with the squire.

"So there we go, boys," said Mr. Dance.

"Come in, Mr. Dance," says the squire, very stately and condescending.

"Good evening, Dance," says the doctor with a nod. "And good evening to you, friend Jim. What good wind brings you here?"

The supervisor stood up straight and stiff and told his story like a lesson.

"Mr. Dance," said the squire, "you are a very noble fellow. This lad Hawkins is a trump, I perceive."

"And so, Jim," said the doctor, "you have the thing that they were after, have you?"

"Here it is, sir," said I, and gave him the oilskin packet.

I made a hearty supper, for I was as hungry as a hawk, while Mr. Dance was further complimented and at last dismissed.

"And now, squire," said the doctor. "You have heard of this Flint, I suppose?"

"Heard of him!" cried the squire. "Heard of him, you say! He was the blood-thirstiest buccaneer that sailed. Blackbeard was a child to Flint."

"What I want to know is this: supposing that I have here in my pocket some clue to where Flint buried his treasure, will that treasure amount to much?"

"It will amount to this: if we have the clue you talk about, I fit out a ship in Bristol dock, and take you and Hawkins here along, and I'll have that treasure if I search a year."

"Very well," said the doctor. "Now, then, if Jim is agreeable, we'll open the packet." The doctor opened the seals with great care, and there fell out the map of an island, with latitude and longitude, soundings, names of hills and bays and inlets, and a hill in the centre part

marked "The Spy-glass."

There were several additions of a later date, but above all, three crosses of red ink—two on the north part of the island, one in the southwest—and beside this last, in the same red ink, and in a small, neat hand, very different from the captain's tottery characters, these words: "Bulk of treasure here."

"Livesey," said the squire, "you will give up this wretched practice at once. Tomorrow I start for Bristol. In three weeks' time—three weeks!—two weeks—ten days—we'll have the best ship, sir, and the choicest crew in England. Hawkins shall come as cabin-boy. You'll make a famous cabin-boy, Hawkins. You, Livesey, are ship's doctor; I am admiral. We'll take Redruth,

Joyce, and Hunter. We'll have favourable winds, a quick passage, and not the least difficulty in finding the spot, and money to eat, to roll in, to play duck and drake with ever after."

✳ ✳ ✳

So the weeks passed on, till one fine day there came a letter addressed to Dr. Livesey.

Old Anchor Inn, Bristol, March 1,

Dear Livesey—The ship is bought and fitted. Two hundred tons; name, Hispaniola. It was the crew that troubled me. I wished a round score of men till the most remarkable stroke of fortune brought me the very man that I required. I was standing on the dock, when, I fell in talk with him. I found he was an old sailor, kept a public-house, knew all the seafaring men in Bristol, had lost his health ashore, and wanted a good berth as cook to get to sea again. I engaged him on the spot to be ship's cook. Long John Silver, he is called, and has lost a leg; but that I regarded as a recommendation, since he lost it in his country's service, under the immortal Hawke. Between Silver and myself we got together in a few days a company of the toughest old salts imaginable—not pretty to look at, but fellows, by their faces, of the most indomitable spirit. Let young Hawkins go at once to see his mother, with Redruth for a guard; and then both come full speed to Bristol.

John Trelawney

I said good-bye to Mother and the cove where I had lived since I was born, and the dear old Admiral Benbow. In Bristol we met Squire Trelawney, all dressed out like a sea-officer, in stout blue cloth.

"Here you are," he cried, "and the doctor came last night from London. Bravo! The ship's company complete! We sail tomorrow!"

Chapter 4

THE VOYAGE

When I had done breakfasting, the squire gave me a note addressed to <u>John Silver</u>, at the sign of the Spy-glass.

Now, to tell you the truth, from the very first mention of Long John in Squire Trelawney's letter I had taken a fear in my mind that he might prove to be the very one-legged sailor whom I had watched for so long at the old Benbow. But one look at the man before me was enough. I had seen the <u>captain,</u> and Black Dog, and the blind man, Pew, and I thought I knew what a buccaneer was like—a very different creature, according to me, from this clean and pleasant-tempered landlord. I would have gone bail for the innocence of Long John Silver.

* * *

The *Hispaniola* lay some way out, and we went under the figureheads and round the sterns of many other ships, and their cables sometimes grated underneath our keel, and sometimes swung above us. At last, however, we got alongside, and were met and saluted as we stepped aboard by the mate, Mr. Arrow, a brown old sailor with earrings in his ears and a squint. He and the squire were very thick and friendly, but I soon observed that things were not the same between Mr. Trelawney and the captain. This last was a sharp-looking man who seemed angry with everything on board and was soon to tell us why.

"Well, Captain Smollett, what have you to say?"

"Well, sir," said the captain, "better speak plain, I believe, even at the risk of offence. I don't like this cruise; I don't like the men; and I don't like my officer. That's short and sweet. I learn we are going after treasure—hear it from my own hands, mind you. Now, treasure is ticklish work; I don't like treasure voyages on any account, and I don't like them, above all, when they are secret and when (begging your pardon, Mr. Trelawney) the secret has been told to the parrot."

"Silver's parrot?" asked the squire.

"It's a way of speaking," said the captain. "Blabbed, I mean. It's my belief neither of you gentlemen know what you are about, but I'll tell you my way of it—life or death, and a close run. There's been too much blabbing already."

"Far too much," agreed the doctor.

"I'll tell you what I've heard myself," continued Captain Smollett, "that you have a map of an island,

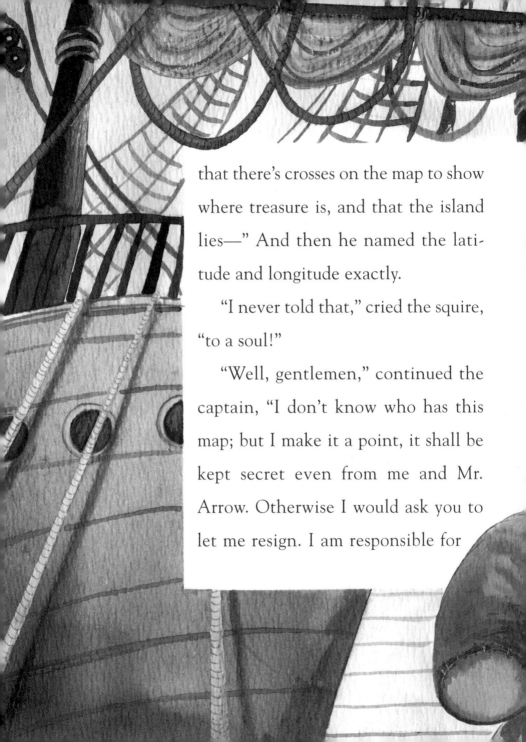

that there's crosses on the map to show where treasure is, and that the island lies—" And then he named the latitude and longitude exactly.

"I never told that," cried the squire, "to a soul!"

"Well, gentlemen," continued the captain, "I don't know who has this map; but I make it a point, it shall be kept secret even from me and Mr. Arrow. Otherwise I would ask you to let me resign. I am responsible for

the ship's safety and the life of every man Jack aboard of her. I see things going, as I think, not quite right. And I ask you to take certain precautions or let me resign my berth. And that's all."

"I will do as you desire," said the squire, "but I think the worse of you."

"That's as you please, sir," said the captain. "You'll find I do my duty."

And with that he took his leave.

Soon the sails began to draw, and the land and shipping to flit by on either side; and before I could lie down to snatch an hour of slumber the *Hispaniola* had begun her voyage to the Isle of Treasure.

✳ ✳ ✳

The coxswain, Israel Hands, was a careful, wily, old, experienced seaman who could be trusted at a pinch with almost anything. He was a great confidant of Long John

Silver, and so the mention of his name leads me on to speak of our ship's cook, Barbecue, as the men called him. To me he was unweariedly kind, and always glad to see me in the galley, which he kept as clean as a new pin, the dishes hanging up burnished and his parrot in a cage in one corner.

"Here's Cap'n Flint—I calls my parrot Cap'n Flint, after the famous buccaneer—here's Cap'n Flint predicting success to our voyage. Wasn't you, cap'n?"

And the parrot would say, with great rapidity, "Pieces of eight! Pieces of eight! Pieces of eight!" till you wondered that it was not out of breath, or till John threw his handkerchief over the cage.

* * *

We had some heavy weather, which only proved the qualities of the *Hispaniola*. Every man on board seemed well content, and they must have been hard to please if they had been otherwise, for it is my belief there was never a ship's company so spoiled since Noah put to sea. Double grog was going on the least excuse; there was duff on odd days, as, for instance, if the squire heard it was any man's birthday, and always a barrel of apples standing broached in the waist for anyone to help himself that had a fancy.

"Never knew good come of it yet," the captain said to Dr. Livesey. "Spoil forecastle hands, make devils. That's my belief."

But good did come of the apple barrel, as you shall hear. It was about the last day of our outward voyage by the largest computation; some time that night, or at latest before noon of the morrow, we should sight the Treasure Island.

Chapter 5

WHAT I HEARD IN THE APPLE BARREL

Now, just after sundown, when all my work was over and I was on my way to my berth, it occurred to me that I should like an apple. I ran on deck. The watch was all forward looking out for the island. In I got bodily into the apple barrel, and found there was scarce an apple left; but sitting down there in the dark, what with the sound of the waters and the rocking movement of the ship, I had either fallen asleep or was on the point of doing so when a heavy man sat down with rather a clash close by.

The barrel shook as he leaned his shoulders against it, and I was about to jump up when the man began to speak. It was Silver's voice, and before I had heard a dozen words, I would not have shown myself for all the world, but lay there, trembling and listening, in the extreme of fear and curiosity, for from these dozen words I understood that the lives of all the honest men aboard depended upon me alone.

"No, not I," said Silver. "Flint was cap'n; I was quartermaster, along of my timber leg. The same broadside I lost my leg, old Pew lost his daylights."

"Ah!" cried another voice, that of the youngest hand on board, and evidently full of admiration. "He was the flower of the flock, was Flint!"

Silver continued, "I laid by two thousand after Flint, that ain't bad for a man before the mast, all safe in a bank."

"But all the other money's gone now, ain't it? You daren't show face in Bristol after this."

"Why, where might you suppose it was?" asked Silver derisively.

"At Bristol, in banks and places," answered his companion. "It were," said the cook; "it were when we weighed anchor. But my old missis has it all by now. And the Spy-glass is sold, lease and goodwill and rigging; and the old girl's off to meet me. I could tell you where, for I trust yer, but it'd make jealousy among the mates."

"Well, I tell you now," replied the lad, "I didn't half a quarter like this job till I had this talk with you, John; but there's my hand on it now."

"And a brave lad you are, and smart too," answered Silver.

By this time I had begun to understand the meaning of their terms, and the little scene that I had overheard was the last act in the corruption of one of the honest hands—perhaps of the last one left aboard. But on this point I was soon to be relieved, for Silver giving a little whistle, a third man strolled up and sat down by the party.

"Dick's square," said Silver.

"Oh, I know'd Dick was square," returned the voice of the coxswain, Israel Hands. "But look here," he went on, "I've had almost enough of Cap'n Smollett; he's hazed me along enough, by thunder!"

"Israel," said Silver, "here's what I say, you'll berth forward, and you'll live hard, and you'll speak soft, and you'll keep sober till I give the word; and you may lay to that, my son."

Just then a sort of brightness fell upon me in the barrel, and looking up, I found the moon had risen and almost at the same time the voice of the lookout shouted, "Land ho!"

There was a great rush of feet across the deck. I could hear people tumbling up from the cabin and the forecastle, and slipping in an instant outside my barrel, I dived behind the fore-sail, and made a double towards the stern, and came out upon the open deck in time to join Hunter and Dr. Livesey in the rush for the weather bow.

"And now, men," said the captain, when all was sheeted home, "has any one of you ever seen that land ahead?"

"I have, sir," said Silver. "I've watered there with a trader I was cook in."

"The anchorage is on the south, behind an islet, I fancy?" asked the captain.

"Yes, sir; Skeleton Island they calls it."

"I have a chart here," said Captain Smollett, "see if that's the place."

Long John's eyes burned in his head as he took the chart, but by the fresh look of the paper I knew he was doomed to disappointment. This was not the map we found in Billy Bones's chest, but an accurate copy, with the single exception of the red crosses and the written notes. Sharp as must have been his annoyance, Silver had the strength of mind to hide it.

Captain Smollett, the squire, and Dr. Livesey were talking together on the quarter-deck. As soon as I was near enough to speak and not to be overheard, I broke immediately, "Doctor, let me speak. Get the captain and squire down to the cabin. I have terrible news."

"Now, Hawkins," said the squire, "you have something to say. Speak up."

I did as I was bid, and as short as I could make it, told the whole details of Silver's conversation.

"First point," began Mr. Smollett. "We must go on, because we can't turn back. If I gave the word to go about, they would rise at once. Second point, we have time before us—at least until this treasure's found. Third point, there are faithful hands."

"Three," reckoned the captain; "ourselves make seven, counting Hawkins here."

"Jim here," said the doctor, "can help us more than anyone. The men are not shy with him, and Jim is a noticing lad."

"Hawkins, I put prodigious faith in you," added the squire.

I began to feel pretty desperate at this, for I felt altogether helpless; and yet, by an odd train of circumstances, it was indeed through me that safety came. In the meantime, talk as we pleased, there were only seven out of the twenty-six on whom we knew we could rely; and out of these seven one was a boy, so that the grown men on our side were six to their nineteen. Mutiny, it was plain, hung over us like a thunder-cloud.

"Let's allow the men an afternoon ashore," said the captain. If they all go, why we'll fight the ship. If they none of them go, well then, we hold the cabin, and God defend the right. If some go, you mark my words, sir, Silver'll bring 'em aboard again as mild as lambs."

It was so decided; loaded pistols were served out to all the sure men; Hunter, Joyce, and Redruth were taken into our confidence and received the news with less surprise and a better spirit than we had looked for, and then the captain went on deck and addressed the crew.

"My lads," said he, "we've had a hot day and are all tired and out of sorts. A turn ashore'll hurt nobody—the boats are still in the water; you can take the gigs, and as many as please may go ashore for the afternoon. I'll fire a gun half an hour before sundown."

Six fellows were to stay on board, and the remaining thirteen, including Silver, began to embark. Then it was that there came into my head the first of the mad notions that contributed so much to save our lives. If six men were left by Silver, it was plain our party could not take and fight the ship; and since only six were left, it was equally plain that the cabin party had no present need of my assistance. It occurred to me at once to go ashore. In a jiffy I had slipped over the side and curled up in the fore-sheets of the nearest boat, and almost at the same moment she shoved off. No one took notice of me, only the bow oar saying, "Is that you, Jim?

Keep your head down." But Silver, from the other boat, looked sharply over and called out to know if that were me; and from that moment I began to regret what I had done.

The crews raced for the beach, but the boat I was in, having some start and being at once the lighter and the better manned, shot far ahead of her consort, and the bow had struck among the shore-side trees and I had caught a branch and swung myself out and

plunged into the nearest thicket while Silver and the rest were still a hundred yards behind.

"Jim, Jim!" I heard him shouting. But you may suppose I paid no heed; jumping, ducking, and breaking through, I ran straight before my nose till I could run no longer.

Chapter 6

THE FIRST BLOW

All at once there began to go a sort of bustle among the bulrushes; a wild duck flew up with a quack, another followed, and soon over the whole surface of the marsh a great cloud of birds hung screaming and circling in the air. I judged at once that some of my shipmates must be drawing near along the borders of the fen. Nor was I deceived, for soon I heard the very distant and low tones of a human voice, which, as I continued to give ear, grew steadily louder and nearer. This put me in a great fear, and I crawled under cover

of the nearest tree and squatted there, hearkening, as silent as a mouse.

Crawling on all fours, I made steadily but slowly towards them, till at last, raising my head to an aperture among the leaves, I could see clear down into a little green dell beside the marsh, and closely set about with trees, where Long John Silver and another of the crew stood face to face in conversation.

"Silver," says he, "as sure as God sees me I'd sooner lose my hand if I turn again my duty."

And then all of a sudden he was interrupted by a noise, a sound like the cry of anger, then another on the back of it; and then one horrid, long-drawn scream.

"In heaven's name, tell me, what was that?" cried the sailor.

"That?" returned Silver, "Oh, I reckon that'll be Alan."

And at this point Tom flashed out like a hero.

"Alan!" he cried. "Then rest his soul for a true sea-man! And as for you, John Silver, long you've been a mate of mine, but you're a mate of mine no more. If I die like a dog, I'll die in my duty. You've killed Alan, have you? Kill me too, if you can. But I defies yer."

And with that, this brave fellow turned his back directly on the cook and set off walking for the beach. But he was not destined to go far. With a cry John seized the branch of a tree, whipped the crutch out of his armpit, and sent that uncouth missile hurtling through the air. It struck poor Tom, point foremost, and with stunning violence, right between the shoulders in the middle of his back. His hands flew up, he gave a sort of gasp, and fell. Silver, agile as a monkey even without leg or crutch, was on the top of him next moment and had twice buried his knife up to the hilt in that defenceless body.

They had already slain two of the honest people; after Tom and Alan, might not I come next?

I ran as I never ran before, scarce minding the direction of my flight, so long as it led me from the murderers; and as I ran, fear grew and grew upon me until it turned into a kind of frenzy. And here a fresh alarm brought me to a standstill with a thumping heart.

From the side of the hill, which was here steep and stony, a spout of gravel was dislodged and fell rattling and bounding through the trees. My eyes turned instinctively in that direction, and I saw a figure leap with great rapidity behind the trunk of a pine. It seemed dark and shaggy; more I knew not. But the terror of this new apparition brought me to a stand.

"Who are you?" I asked.

"Ben Gunn," he answered, and his voice sounded hoarse and awkward, like a rusty lock. "I'm poor Ben

Gunn, I am; and I haven't spoke with a Christian these three years."

"Three years!" I cried. "Were you shipwrecked?"

"Nay, mate," said he; "Marooned. Marooned three years agone," he continued, "and lived on goats since then, and berries, and oysters. Now you, what do you call yourself mate?"

"Jim," I told him.

"Jim, I'm rich. Rich! I says. And I'll tell you what, I'll make a man of you, Jim. Ah, Jim, you'll bless your stars, you will, you was the first that found me! Now, Jim, you tell me true, that ain't Flint's ship?" he asked.

"It's not Flint's ship, and Flint is dead; but I'll tell you true, as you ask me—there are some of Flint's hands aboard; worse luck for the rest of us."

"Not a man—with one—leg?" he gasped.

I had made up my mind in a moment, and by way of answer told him the whole story of our voyage and the predicament in which we found ourselves. He heard me with the keenest interest, and when I had done he patted me on the head.

"Now, I'll tell you what," he went on. "I were in Flint's ship when he buried the treasure.

Billy Bones was the mate; Long John, he was quarter-master; and they asked him where the treasure was. 'Ah,' says he, 'you can go ashore, if you like, and stay, he says; 'but as for the ship, she'll beat up for more, by thunder!' That's what he said. Well, I was in another ship three years back, and we sighted this island. 'Boys,' said I, 'here's Flint's treasure; let's land and find it.' Twelve days they looked for it, and every day they had the worse word for me, until one fine morning all hands went aboard. 'As for you, Benjamin Gunn,' says they, 'here's a musket,' they says, 'and a spade, and a pick-axe. You can stay here and find Flint's money for yourself,' they says. Well, Jim, three years have I been here, and not a bite of Christian diet from that day to this. But now, you look here; look at me. Do I look like a man before the mast? No, says you. Nor I weren't, neither, I says. Just you mention them words to your squire, Jim," he went on.

"But how am I to get on board?"

"Ah," said he, "Well, there's my boat, that I made with my two hands. I keep her under the white rock. Hi!" he broke out. "What's that?"

For just then, all the echoes of the island awoke and bellowed to the thunder of a cannon.

"They've begun to fight!" I cried. "Follow me."

And I began to run towards the anchorage, my terrors all forgotten, while close at my side the marooned man in his goatskins trotted easily and lightly. The cannon-shot was followed after a considerable interval by a volley of small arms. Another pause, and then, not a quarter of a mile in front of me, I beheld the Union Jack flutter in the air above a wood.

Chapter 7

NARRATIVE CONTINUED BY THE DOCTOR: HOW THE SHIP WAS ABANDONED

It was about half past one when the two boats went ashore from the *Hispaniola*. The captain, the squire, and I were talking matters over in the cabin. Waiting was a strain, and it was decided that Hunter and I should go ashore with the jolly-boat in quest of information.

Hunter and I pulled straight in, in the direction of the stockade upon the chart. There was a slight bend in the coast, and I steered so as to put it between us; even before we landed we had thus lost sight of the gigs. I jumped out and came as near running as I durst, with a big silk handkerchief under my hat for coolness' sake and a brace of pistols ready primed for safety. I had not gone a hundred yards when I reached the stockade.

This was how it was; a spring of clear water rose almost at the top of a knoll. Well, on the knoll, and enclosing the spring, they'd clapped a stout log-house fit to hold two score of people on a pinch and loop-holed for musketry on either side. All round this they'd cleared a wide space, and then the thing was completed by a paling six feet high, without door or opening, too strong to pull down without time and labour and too open to shelter the besiegers. The people in the log-house had them in every way; they stood quiet in shelter and shot the others like partridges. Short of a complete surprise, they might have held the place against a regiment.

What particularly took my fancy was the spring. For though we had a good enough place of it in the cabin of the *Hispaniola*, with plenty of arms and ammunition, and things to eat, and excellent wines, there had been one thing overlooked—we had no water. I was thinking this over when there came ringing over the island the cry of a man at the point of death. "Jim Hawkins is gone," was my first thought. Now I made up my mind instantly, and with no time lost returned to the shore and jumped on board the jolly-boat.

The boat was soon alongside and I aboard the schooner. I told my plan to the captain, and between us we settled on the details of its accomplishment. Hunter brought the boat round under the stern-port, and Joyce and I set to work loading her with powder tins, muskets, bags of biscuits, kegs of pork, a cask of cognac, and my invaluable medicine chest.

In the meantime, the squire and the captain stayed on deck, and the latter hailed the coxswain, who was the principal man aboard.

"Mr. Hands," he said, "here are two of us with a brace of pistols each. If any one of you six make a signal of any description, that man's dead."

They were a good deal taken aback and we heard no more, for the time, of these six very faint-hearted seamen.

We had soon touched land in the same place as before and set to provision the block house. So we proceeded without pausing to take breath, till the whole cargo was bestowed, and I, with all my power, sculled back to the

Hispaniola. The squire was waiting for me at the stern window, and we fell to loading the boat for our very lives.

✳ ✳ ✳

We put the boat's head direct for the landing-place. We waded ashore as fast as we could. Forty paces farther we came to the edge of the wood and saw the stockade in front of us. We struck the enclosure about the middle of the south side, and almost at the same time, seven mutineers appeared in full cry at the south-western corner. They paused as if taken aback, and before they recovered, not only the squire and I, but Hunter and Joyce from the block house, had time to fire. The four shots came in rather a scattering volley, but they did the business: one of the enemy actually fell, and the rest, without hesitation, turned and plunged into the trees.

We began to rejoice over our good success when just at that moment a pistol cracked in the bush, a ball

whistled close past my ear, and poor Tom Redruth stumbled and fell his length on the ground and I saw with half an eye that all was over. We laid him down in the log-house to die.

"Somebody hailing us," said Hunter, who was on guard.

"Doctor! Squire! Captain! Hullo, Hunter, is that you?" came the cries. And I ran to the door in time to see Jim Hawkins, safe and sound, come climbing over the stockade.

Chapter 8

Narrative Resumed by Jim Hawkins

The *Hispaniola* still lay where she had anchored; but, sure enough, there was the Jolly Roger—the black flag of piracy—flying from her peak. At length I thought I might return towards the stockade. I skirted among the woods until I had regained the rear, or shoreward side, of the stockade, and was soon warmly welcomed by the faithful party and I had soon told my story.

"Is this Ben Gunn a man?" asked the doctor.

"I do not know, sir," said I. "I am not very sure whether he's sane."

Our best hope, it was decided, was to kill off the buccaneers until they either hauled down their flag or ran away with the *Hispaniola*. From nineteen they were already reduced to fifteen, two others were wounded, and one at least, severely wounded, if he were not dead. And besides that, we had two able allies—rum and the climate. As for the first, though we were about half a mile away, we could hear them roaring and singing late into the night; and as for the second, the doctor staked his wig that, camped where they were in the marsh and unprovided with remedies, the half of them would be on their backs before a week.

The next morning I was wakened by a bustle and the sound of voices.

"Flag of truce!" I heard someone say; and then, immediately after, with a cry of surprise, "Silver himself!"

"Keep indoors, men," said the captain. "Ten to one this is a trick. My man," said Captain Smollett, "I have not the slightest desire to talk to you. If you wish to talk to me, you can come, that's all. If there's any treachery, it'll be on your side, and the Lord help you."

"Well, here it is," said Silver. "We want that treasure, and we'll have it—that's our point! You would just as soon save your lives, I reckon; and that's yours. You have a chart, haven't you?"

"That's as may be," replied the captain.

"You give us the chart to get the treasure by, and we'll offer you a choice. Either you come aboard along of us, once the treasure's shipped, and then I'll give you my affy-davy, upon my word of honour, to clap you somewhere safe ashore. Or if that ain't to your fancy, some of my hands being rough and having old scores on account of hazing, then you can stay here, you can."

Captain Smollett rose from his seat and knocked out the ashes of his pipe in the palm of his left hand.

"Is that all?" he asked.

"Every last word, by thunder!" answered John. "Refuse that, and you've seen the last of me but musket-balls."

"Very good," said the captain. "Now you'll hear me. If you'll come up one by one, unarmed, I'll engage to clap you all in irons and take you home to a fair trial in England. If you won't, my name is Alexander Smollett, I've flown my sovereign's colours, and I'll see you all to Davy Jones. You can't find the treasure. You can't sail the ship—there's not a man among you fit to sail the ship."

Silver's face was a picture; his eyes started in his head with wrath. Then he spat into the spring. And with a dreadful oath he stumbled off, and disappeared in an instant afterwards among the trees.

As soon as Silver disappeared, the captain, who had been closely watching him, turned towards the interior of the house.

"My lads," said he, "I've given Silver a broadside. I pitched it in red-hot on purpose; and before the hour's out, we shall be boarded. We're outnumbered, I needn't tell you that, but we fight in shelter; and a minute ago I should have said we fought with discipline. I've no manner of doubt that we can drub them, if you choose."

An hour passed away, till suddenly Joyce whipped up his musket and fired. The report had scarcely died away ere it was repeated and repeated from without in a scattering volley, shot behind shot, like a string of geese, from every side of the enclosure. Then with a loud huzza, a little cloud of pirates leaped from the woods on the north side and ran straight on the stockade. The boarders swarmed over the fence like monkeys and the head of Job Anderson, the boatswain, appeared at the middle loophole.

"At 'em, all hands!" he roared in a voice of thunder.

At the same moment, another pirate grasped Hunter's musket by the muzzle, wrenched it from his hands, and with one stunning blow, laid the poor fellow senseless on the floor. Meanwhile a third, appeared suddenly in the doorway and fell with his cutlass on the doctor.

"Out, lads, out, and fight 'em in the open! Cutlasses!" cried the captain.

I snatched a cutlass from the pile, and someone, at the same time snatching another, gave me a cut across

the knuckles which I hardly felt. I dashed out of the door into the clear sunlight. Right in front, the doctor was pursuing his assailant down the hill, and just as my eyes fell upon him, beat down his guard and sent him sprawling on his back with a great slash across the face.

"Round the house, lads! Round the house!" cried the captain; and even in the hurly-burly, I perceived a change in his voice. Next moment I was face to face with Anderson. He roared aloud and his hanger went up above his head, flashing in the sunlight. I had not time to be afraid, but as the blow still hung impending, leaped in a trice upon one side, and missing my foot in the soft sand rolled headlong down the slope. And yet, in this breath of time, the fight was over and the victory was ours.

Gray, following close behind me, had cut down the big boatswain ere he had time to recover from his last blow. Another had been shot at a loophole in the very act of firing into the house and now lay in agony, the pistol still smoking in his hand. A third, as I had seen, the doctor had disposed of at a blow.

We saw at a glance the price we had paid for victory. Hunter lay beside his loophole, stunned; Joyce by his, shot through the head, never to move again; while right in the centre, the squire was supporting the captain, one as pale as the other.

"The captain's wounded," said Mr. Trelawney.

"Have they run?" asked Mr. Smollett.

"All that could, you may be bound," returned the doctor; "but there's five of them will never run again."

"Five!" cried the captain. "Come, that's better. Five against three leaves us four to nine. That's better odds than we had at starting.

Chapter 9

HOW MY SEA ADVENTURE BEGAN

There was no return of the mutineers, not so much as another shot out of the woods. As for the captain, his wounds were grievous indeed, but not dangerous. No organ was fatally injured.

It being then a little past noon, the doctor took up his hat and pistols, girt on a cutlass, put the chart in his pocket, and with a musket over his shoulder crossed the palisade on the north side and set off briskly through the trees.

"I take it," says I, "the doctor has his idea; and if I am right, he's going now to see Ben Gunn."

The house being stifling hot and the little patch of sand inside the palisade ablaze with midday sun, I began to envy the doctor walking in the cool shadow of the woods. Being near a bread-bag, and no one then observing me, I took the first steps towards my escapade and filled both pockets of my coat with biscuit. The next thing I laid hold of was a brace of pistols, and as I already had a powder-horn and bullets, I felt myself well supplied with arms. I made a bolt for it over the stockade and into the thickest of the trees, and before my absence was observed I was out of cry of my companions. It was already late in the afternoon, although still warm and sunny.

I walked along beside the surf with great enjoyment, till I took the cover of some thick bushes and crept warily up to the ridge of the spit. Behind me was the sea, in front the anchorage. The *Hispaniola*, in that unbroken mirror, was exactly portrayed from the truck to the waterline, the Jolly Roger hanging from her peak. Alongside lay one of the gigs, Silver in the stern-sheets—him I could always recognize—while a couple of men were leaning over the stern bulwarks. All at once there began the most horrid, unearthly screaming, which at first startled me badly, though I had soon remembered the voice of Captain Flint and even thought I could make out the bird by her bright plumage as she sat perched upon her master's wrist. Soon after, the jolly-boat shoved off and pulled for shore, and the two men went below by the cabin companion. Just about the same time, it began to grow dark. I saw I must lose no time for I had decided to try to find Ben Gunn's boat.

The white rock, visible enough above the brush, was still some eighth of a mile further down the spit. Right

below it there was an exceedingly small hollow of green turf, and in the centre of the dell, sure enough, a little tent of goat-skins. I dropped into the hollow, lifted the side of the tent, and there was Ben Gunn's boat; a rude, lop-sided frame-work of tough wood, and stretched upon that a covering of goat-skin, with the hair inside. Well, now that I had found the boat, you

would have thought that I had had enough of truancy for once, but in the meantime I had taken another notion. This was to slip out under cover of the night, cut the *Hispaniola* adrift, and let her go ashore where she fancied.

The coracle, as I had ample reason to know before I was done with her, was a very safe boat for a person of my height and weight, both buoyant and clever in a sea-way; but she was the most cross-grained, lop-sided craft to manage. By good fortune, paddle as I pleased, the tide was still sweeping me down; and there lay the *Hispaniola* right in the fairway, hardly to be missed.

First she loomed before me like a blot of something yet blacker than darkness, then her spars and hull began to take shape, and the next moment, as it seemed, I was alongside of her hawser and had laid hold. I felt the hawser slacken in my grasp. With that I made my mind up, took out my gully, opened it with my teeth, and cut one strand after another, till the vessel swung only by two. Then I lay quiet, waiting to sever these last when the strain should once more be lightened by a breath of wind.

At last the breeze came; I felt the hawser slacken once more, and with a good effort, cut the last fibres through. I was surprised by a sudden lurch of the coracle. The current had turned at right angles, sweeping round along with it the tall schooner and the little dancing coracle; it went spinning through the narrows for the open sea. I lay down flat in the bottom of that wretched skiff and devoutly recommended my spirit to its Maker.

So I must have lain for hours, continually beaten to and fro upon the billows, until sleep at last supervened and in my sea-tossed coracle I lay and dreamed of home and the old Admiral Benbow.

* * *

It was broad day when I awoke and found myself tossing at the south-west end of Treasure Island.

"Well, now," thought I to myself, "it is plain I must lie where I am and not disturb the balance; but it is plain also that I can put the paddle over the side and from time to time, in smooth places, give her a shove or two towards land."

It was very tiring and slow work, but the current had soon carried me past the point, and as the next reach of sea opened out, I beheld a sight that changed the nature of my thoughts.

Right in front of me, not half a mile away, I beheld the *Hispaniola* under sail. It became plain to me that nobody was steering. And if so, where were the men? Either they were dead drunk or had deserted her, I thought, and perhaps if I could get on board I might return the vessel to her captain. I set myself, with all my strength and caution, to paddle after the unsteered *Hispaniola* and gradually I got into the way of the thing and guided my coracle among the waves. But now, at last, I had my chance. The breeze fell for some seconds, very low, and the current gradually turning her, the *Hispaniola* revolved slowly round her centre and at last presented me her stern, with the cabin window still gaping open and the lamp over the table still burning on into the day. I sprang to my feet and leaped, stamping the coracle under water. With one hand I caught the jib-boom, while my foot was lodged between the stay and the brace; and as I still clung there panting, a dull blow told me that the schooner had charged down upon and struck the coracle and

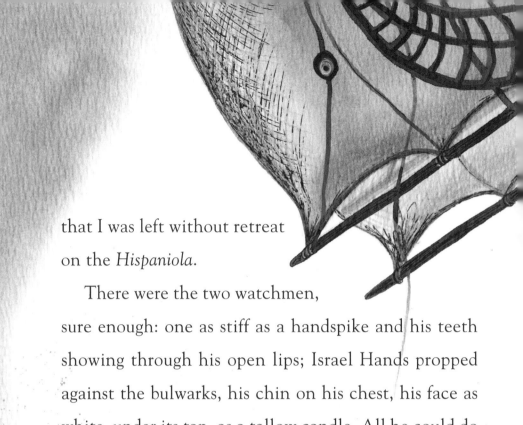

that I was left without retreat
on the *Hispaniola*.

There were the two watchmen,
sure enough: one as stiff as a handspike and his teeth
showing through his open lips; Israel Hands propped
against the bulwarks, his chin on his chest, his face as
white, under its tan, as a tallow candle. All he could do
was to utter one word, "Brandy."

It occurred to me there was no time to lose, I slipped aft and down the companion stairs into the cabin. All the lockfast places had been broken open in quest of the chart. I went into the cellar; all the barrels were gone, and of the bottles a most surprising number had been drunk out and thrown away. Certainly, since the mutiny began, not a man of them could ever have been sober. Foraging about, I found a bottle with some brandy left, for Hands and went back to him.

"Well," said I, "I've come aboard to take possession of this ship, Mr. Hands; and you'll please regard me as your captain until further notice. I mean to get into North Inlet and beach her quietly there."

"I've tried my fling, I have, and I've lost, and it's you has the wind of me. North Inlet? Why, I haven't no choice, not I! I'd help you sail her up to Execution Dock, by thunder! So I would."

Well, as it seemed to me, there was some sense in this. We struck our bargain on the spot. In three minutes I had the *Hispaniola* sailing easily before the wind along the coast of Treasure Island, with good hopes of turning the northern point ere noon and beating down again as far as North Inlet before high water, when we might beach her safely and wait till the subsiding tide permitted us to land.

Chapter 10

ON PAROLE

The excitement of these last manoeuvres had somewhat interfered with the watch I had kept hitherto, sharply enough, upon the coxswain. Perhaps I'd heard a creak or saw his shadow moving with the tail of my eye; perhaps it was an instinct like a cat's; but, sure enough, when I looked round, there was Hands, already half-way towards me, with a dirk in his right hand. He threw himself forward and I leapt sideways towards the bows. As I did so, I let go of the tiller, which sprang sharp to leeward, and I think this saved my life, for it struck Hands across the chest and stopped him, for the moment, dead. Before he could recover, I was safe out of the corner where he had me trapped, with all the deck to dodge about. Just forward of the main-mast I stopped, drew a pistol from my pocket, took a cool aim, and drew the trigger. The hammer fell, but there followed neither flash nor sound; the priming was useless with sea-water.

While things stood thus, suddenly the *Hispaniola* struck, staggered, ground for an instant in the sand, and then, swift as a blow, canted over to the port side till the deck stood at an angle of forty-five degrees. Quick as thought, I sprang into the mizzen shrouds, rattled up hand over hand, and did not draw a breath till I was seated on the cross-trees. I lost no time in changing the priming of my pistol, and then, having one ready for service, and to make assurance doubly sure, I proceeded to draw the load of the other and recharge it afresh from the beginning.

Hands also hauled himself heavily into the shrouds, and with the dirk in his teeth, began slowly and painfully to mount.

"One more step, Mr. Hands," said I, "and I'll blow your brains out!"

Back went his right hand over his shoulder. Something sang like an arrow through the air; I felt a blow and then a sharp pang, and there I was pinned by the shoulder to the mast. In the horrid pain and surprise of the moment both my pistols went off, and both escaped out of my hands. They did not fall alone; with a choked cry, the coxswain loosed his grasp upon the shrouds and plunged head first into the water.

The hot blood was running over my back and chest. The dirk, where it had pinned my shoulder to the mast, seemed to burn like a hot iron. It was my first thought to pluck forth the dirk, but either it stuck too hard or my nerve failed me, and I desisted with a violent shudder. Oddly enough, that very shudder did the business. The knife, in fact, had come the nearest in the world to missing me altogether; it held me by a mere pinch of skin, and this the shudder tore

away. The blood ran down the faster, to be sure, but I was my own master again and only tacked to the mast by my coat and shirt.

It began to be chill; the tide was rapidly fleeting seaward, and holding the cut hawser in both hands for a last security, I let myself drop softly overboard and I waded ashore in great spirits and set my face homeward for the blockhouse and my companions.

Sometimes walking, sometimes running, I drew impatiently towards my goal. All was dark within, so that I could distinguish nothing by the eye. With my arms before me I walked steadily in. And then, all of a sudden, a shrill voice broke forth out of the darkness:

"Pieces of eight! Pieces of eight! Pieces of eight! Pieces of eight! Pieces of eight!"

Silver's green parrot, Captain Flint! I had no time left me to recover. At the sharp, clipping tone of the

parrot, the sleepers
awoke and sprang up;
and with a mighty oath, the
voice of Silver cried, "Who goes?"

The pirates were in possession of the house and stores.
There were six of the buccaneers, all told; not another
man was left alive. The parrot sat, preening her plumage,
on Long John's shoulder.

"So," said he, "here's Jim Hawkins, shiver my timbers!
Dropped in, like, eh? Well, come, I take that friendly.
Yesterday morning, Mr. Hawkins," said he, "in the dog-
watch, down came Doctor Livesey with a flag of truce.

Says he, 'Cap'n Silver, you're sold out. Ship's gone. Well,' says the doctor, 'let's bargain.' We bargained, him and I, and here we are: stores, brandy, blockhouse, and in a manner of speaking, the whole blessed boat, from cross-trees to kelson. As for them, they've tramped; I don't know where's they are."

"As for the schooner," I said, "it was I who cut her cable. Kill me, if you please, or spare me. But one thing I'll say, and no more; if you spare me, bygones are bygones, and when you fellows are in court for piracy, I'll save you all I can. It's for you to choose. Kill another and do yourselves no good, or spare me and keep a witness to save you from the gallows."

"Understand me, Jim," Silver said, "I've a head on my shoulders, I have. I'm on squire's side now. I know you've got that ship safe somewheres. I know when a game's up, I do; and I know a lad that's staunch. Ah, you that's young, you and me might have done a power of good together!"

That was the end of the night's business. Soon after, with a drink all round, we lay down to sleep.

* * *

I was wakened, indeed, we were all wakened, for I could see even the sentinel shake himself together from where he had fallen against the door-post, by a clear, hearty voice hailing us from the margin of the wood:

"Blockhouse, ahoy!" it cried. "Here's the doctor."

And the doctor it was.

"You, doctor! Top o' the morning to you, sir!" cried Silver, "We've quite a surprise for you, sir," he continued.

"Not Jim?"

"The very same Jim as ever was," says Silver.

"Well, well," he said at last, "I should wish to have a talk with that boy, please."

Very deliberately, then, did we advance across the sand to where the doctor awaited us on the other side of the stockade, and as soon as we were within easy speaking distance Silver stopped and stepped back a little way, till he was out of earshot.

Rapidly I described to him my adventures, and he heard me out in silence.

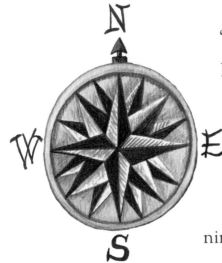

"There is a kind of fate in this," he observed when I had done. "You found out the plot; you found Ben Gunn, the best deed that ever you did, or will do, though you live to ninety. Silver!" he cried. "I'll give you a piece of advice, don't you be in any great hurry after that treasure."

"I can only, asking your pardon, save my life and the boy's by seeking for that treasure; and you may lay to that."

"Well, Silver," replied the doctor, "if that is so, I'll go one step further, look out for squalls when you find it."

And Dr. Livesey shook hands with me through the stockade, nodded to Silver, and set off at a brisk pace into the wood.

"And now, Jim, we're to go in for this here treasure-hunting, and you and me must stick close, back to back like, and we'll save our necks in spite o' fate and fortune."

Chapter 11

THE TREASURE-HUNT

a mystery that still hung over the behaviour of my friends, their unexplained desertion of the stockade, their inexplicable cession of the chart, or harder still to understand, the doctor's last warning to Silver, "Look out for squalls when you find it," and you will readily believe how little taste I found in my breakfast and with how uneasy a heart I set forth behind my captors on the quest for treasure. The party spread itself abroad, in a fan shape, shouting and leaping to and fro.

We had thus proceeded for about half a mile and were approaching the brow of the plateau when the man upon the farthest left began to cry aloud, as if in terror. Shout after shout came from him, and the others began to run in his direction.

At the foot of a pretty big pine and involved in a green creeper, which had even partly lifted some of the smaller bones, a human skeleton lay, with a few shreds of clothing, on the ground. I believe a chill struck for a moment to every heart. On a second glance, it seemed impossible to fancy that the body was in a natural position. But for some disarray the man lay perfectly straight, his feet pointing in one direction, his hands, raised above his head like a diver's, pointing directly in the opposite.

"I've taken a notion into my old numbskull," observed Silver. "Here's the compass; there's the tip-top point o' Skeleton Island, stickin' out like a tooth. Just take a bearing, will you, along the line of them bones."

It was done. The body pointed straight in the direction of the island, and the compass read duly E.S.E. and by E as instructed by the chart.

"There are three tall trees," said he, "about in the right line from Skeleton Island. Spy-glass shoulder I take it, means that lower point there. It's child's play to find the stuff now. I've half a mind to dine first."

All of a sudden, out of the middle of the trees in front of us, a thin, high, trembling voice struck up the well-known air and words:

"Fifteen men on the dead man's chest—

Yo-ho-ho, and a bottle of rum!"

I have never seen men more dreadfully affected than the pirates. The colour went from their six faces like en-chantment; some leaped to their feet, some clawed hold of others:

"It's Flint, by—" cried one.

"Come," said Silver, struggling with his ashen lips to get the word out; "this won't do. Stand by to go about. This is a rum start, and I can't name the voice, but it's someone skylarking, someone that's flesh and blood, and you may lay to that."

His courage had come back as he spoke, and some of the colour to his face along with it. "Shipmates," he cried, "I'm here to get that stuff, and I'll not be beat by man or devil. I never was feared of Flint in his life, and, by the powers, I'll face him dead. There's seven hundred thousand pound not a quarter of a mile from here. When did ever a gentleman o' fortune show his stern to that much dollars for a boozy old seaman with a blue mug, and him dead too? It was liker somebody else's voice now—it was liker— By the powers, Ben Gunn!" roared Silver.

It was extraordinary how their spirits returned and how the natural colour had revived in their faces. Dead or alive, nobody minded Ben Gunn.

The first of the tall trees was reached, and by the bearings proved the wrong one. So with the second. The third rose nearly two hundred feet into the air above a clump of underwood, a giant of a vegetable, with a red column as big as a cottage, and a wide shadow around in which a company could have manoeuvred.

Silver hobbled, grunting, on his crutch. I could not doubt that he hoped to seize upon the treasure, find and board the *Hispaniola* under cover of night, cut every honest throat about that island, and sail away as he had at first intended, laden with crimes and riches.

We were now at the margin of the thicket. And suddenly, not ten yards further, we beheld them stop. A low cry arose. Before us was a great excavation, not very recent, for the sides had fallen in and grass had sprouted on the bottom. The cache had been found and rifled; the seven hundred thousand pounds were gone!

Chapter 12

THE FALL OF A CHIEFTAIN

There never was such an overturn in this world. The buccaneers, with oaths and cries, began to leap, one after another, into the pit and to dig with their fingers, throwing the boards aside as they did so. But just then—crack! crack! crack! Three musket-shots flashed out of the thicket. One of the men spun round like a tee-totum and fell all his length upon his side, where he lay dead, but still twitching; and the other three turned and ran for it with all their might. At the same moment, the doctor, Gray, and Ben Gunn joined us, with smoking muskets, from among the nutmeg-trees.

"Forward!" cried the doctor. "Double quick, my lads. We must head 'em off the boats."

And we set off at a great pace, sometimes plunging through the bushes to the chest. I tell you, but Silver was anxious to keep up with us. As it was, he was already thirty yards behind us and on the verge of strangling when we reached the brow of the slope.

"Doctor," he hailed, "see there! No hurry!"

Sure enough there was no hurry. In a more open part of the plateau, we could see the three survivors still running in the same direction as they had started, right for Mizzen-mast Hill. We were already between them and the boats; and so we four sat down to breathe, while Long John, mopping his face, came slowly up with us.

"Thank ye kindly, doctor," says he. "You came in in about the nick, I guess, for me and Hawkins. And so it's you, Ben Gunn!" he added. "Well, you're a nice one, to be sure."

"I'm Ben Gunn, I am," replied the maroon, wriggling like an eel in his embarrassment. "And," he added, after a long pause, "how do, Mr. Silver? Pretty well, I thank ye, says you."

"Ben, Ben," murmured Silver, "to think as you've done me!"

Ben, in his long, lonely wanderings about the island, had found the skeleton—it was he that had rifled it; he had found the treasure; he had dug it up; he had carried it on his back, in many weary journeys, from the foot of the tall pine to a cave he had on the two-pointed hill at the north-east angle of the island, and there it had lain stored in safety since two months before the arrival of the *Hispaniola*. When the doctor had wormed this secret from him on the afternoon of the attack, and when next morning he saw the anchorage deserted, he had gone to Silver, given him the chart, which was now useless, given him the stores, for Ben Gunn's cave was well supplied with goats' meat salted by himself—given anything and everything to get a chance of moving in safety from the stockade to the two-pointed hill, there to be clear of malaria and to keep a guard upon the money.

"Ah," said Silver, "it were fortunate for me that I had Hawkins here. You would have let old John be cut to bits, and never given it a thought, doctor."

"Not a thought," replied Dr. Livesey cheerily.

And by this time we had reached the gigs. The doctor, with the pick-axe, demolished one of them, and then we all got aboard the other and set out to go round by sea for North Inlet. Just inside the mouth of North Inlet, what should we meet but the *Hispaniola*, cruising by herself? There was little amiss beyond the wreck of the main-sail. Another anchor was got ready and dropped in a fathom and a half of water. We all pulled round again to Rum Cove, the nearest point for Ben Gunn's treasure-house; and then Gray, single-handed, returned with the gig to the *Hispaniola*, where he was to pass the night on guard.

A gentle slope ran up from the beach to the entrance of the cave. At the top,

the squire met us. And thereupon we all entered the cave. It was a large, airy place, with a little spring and a pool of clear water, overhung with ferns. Before a big fire lay Captain Smollett; and in a far corner, only duskily flickered over by the blaze, I beheld great heaps of coin and quadrilaterals built of bars of gold. That was Flint's treasure that we had come so far to seek and that had cost already the lives of seventeen men from the *Hispaniola*.

What a supper I had of it that night, with all my friends around me; and what a meal it was, with Ben Gunn's salted goat and some delicacies and a bottle of old wine from the *Hispaniola*. Never, I am sure, were people gayer or happier. And there was Silver, sitting back almost out of the firelight, but eating heartily, prompt to spring forward when anything was wanted, even joining quietly in our laughter—the same bland, polite, obsequious seaman of the voyage out.

* * *

The next morning we fell early to work, for the transportation of this great mass of gold near a mile by land to the beach, and thence three miles by boat to the *Hispaniola*, was a considerable task for so small a number of workmen. The three fellows still abroad upon the island did not greatly trouble us. A council was held, and it was decided that we must desert them on the island, to the huge glee, I must say, of Ben Gunn. We left a good stock of powder and shot, the bulk of the salt goat, a few medicines, and some other necessaries, tools, clothing, a spare sail, a fathom or two of rope, and by the particular desire of the doctor, a handsome present of tobacco.

And at last, one fine morning, we weighed anchor, which was about all that we could manage, and stood out of North Inlet, the same colours flying that the captain had flown and fought under at the palisade.

We laid her head for the nearest port in Spanish America, for we could not risk the voyage home without fresh hands. Here we met the captain of an English man-of-war, fell in talk with him, went on board his ship, and, in short, had so agreeable a time, that day was breaking when we came alongside the *Hispaniola*. Ben Gunn was on deck alone, and as soon as we came on board he began, with wonderful contortions, to make us a confession. Silver was gone. The maroon had connived at his escape in a shore boat some hours ago, and he now assured us he had only done so to preserve our lives, which would certainly have been forfeit if "that man with the one leg had stayed aboard." But this was not all. The sea-cook had not gone empty-handed. He had cut through a bulkhead unobserved and had removed one of the sacks of coin, worth perhaps three or four hundred guineas, to help him on his further wanderings.

I think we were all pleased to be so cheaply quit of him.

Well, to make a long story short, we got a few hands on board, made a good cruise home, and the *Hispaniola* reached Bristol. Five men only of those who had sailed returned with her.

All of us had an ample share of the treasure and used it wisely or foolishly, according to our natures. As for Ben Gunn, he got a thousand pounds, which he spent or lost in three weeks, or to be more exact, in nineteen days,

for he was back begging on the twentieth. Then he was given a lodge to keep, and he still lives, a great favourite, though something of a butt, with the country boys, and a notable singer in church on Sundays and saints' days.

Of Silver we have heard no more. That formidable seafaring man with one leg has at last gone clean out of my life.

Oxen and wain-ropes would not bring me back again to that accursed island; and the worst dreams that ever I have are when I hear the surf booming about its coasts or start upright in bed with the sharp voice of Captain Flint still ringing in my ears: "Pieces of eight! Pieces of eight!"

ABOUT THE AUTHOR

Robert Louis Stevenson was born on November 13, 1850, in Scotland. His father was a lighthouse builder, which prompted Robert to pursue engineering at Edinburgh University when he was 16 years old. He later changed his focus to law, but could not help that he greatly enjoyed writing more than anything. He eventually left his career in law to follow his dreams of publishing literature. *Treasure Island* was his first major success and one of his best-known works.